Teaching
Others
And
Demonstrating _____.

This book aims to provide children with a framework and language to develop a foundation of strong character as they begin to navigate everyday life.

Practicing virtues and embracing T.O.A.D (Teaching Others And Demonstrating) is essential in everyday life. Virtues like kindness, compassion, integrity, and empathy shape our interactions, fostering connection, trust, and personal fulfillment. Sharing virtues with others inspires positive change and creates a more compassionate society. Let's bring the magic of T.O.A.D into our lives and make a difference in the world.

Teaching
Others
And
Demonstrating _____.
(YOU FILL IN THE VIRTUE OF WHAT YOU
WANT TO DEMONSTRATE)

JJ's TOAD-ALLY GREAT ADVENTURE

WRITTEN BY
JOE SWEENEY

This book is dedicated to my army of amphibians at home, my wife Melissa, and my four kids, JJ, Mackenzie, Mia, and Ryan. Thank you for always believing in me and allowing me to **T**each **O**thers **A**nd **D**emonstrate what it means to make a difference in someone's life every day!

THIS BOOK BELONGS TO:

_____

JJ was happiest when he was outside exploring, looking for bugs and any other fantastic creatures.

It was a late summer afternoon, and JJ was lifting rock after rock, finding creatures like rolly-pollies and worms.

JJ was so excited! When he found it, he came running to his dad with the toad in his hand, shouting, "Daddy, look what I found!"

JJ's dad quickly told him to put it in his bug catcher and gather some supplies for his temporary cage.

JJ and his friend, Ryan, found sticks and even put a little water feeder in the cage.

As the sun began to set for the evening, JJ's dad said it was bath time. JJ was sad that he wasn't going to be able to play outside anymore.

JJ's dad said, "Let's put the toad on the front doorstep, so it gets some fresh air."

JJ was hesitant because he didn't want him to be lonely but found the perfect spot to place the bug catcher.

As bath time finished up, JJ sprinted downstairs so he could check on his toad.

As he looked out the window, JJ noticed the toad and bug catcher were not there.

JJ was sad when he discovered that Ryan had taken it off the doorstep and brought it to his house.

JJ was so angry at his friend and asked his dad to call Ryan's dad to get it back.

His dad explained that sometimes these things happen and he will find him a new toad. JJ's dad told him he needed to forgive his friend, Ryan, and everything would be okay.

JJ chose to forgive Ryan. They would always be friends.

One night, JJ's dad took a neighborhood walk with his dog, Sadie. As he was walking, a toad hopped in front of him onto the sidewalk. JJ's dad quickly grabbed the toad and took it home.

As he got home, he attempted to put Sadie in the house while still holding the toad. JJ's dad placed the toad on a rocking chair, on the doorstep. As he looked down, the toad hopped three times into the bushes.

JJ's dad was so disappointed that the toad got away, and he was not going to be able to show JJ. When he brought the dog into the house, he decided to go back outside and look in the bushes for the toad.

HONEY!

As JJ's dad lifted the branches of the bush, he saw the toad sitting there. JJ's dad was so happy he quickly grabbed the toad and ran into the house, yelling at JJ's mom to get the bug catcher. JJ's dad placed the toad into the bug catcher and put it in the backyard for JJ.

The following morning, JJ woke up as his dad was getting ready for work. When JJ woke up that morning, he was kind of grumpy, his dad noticed.

JJ's dad said, "JJ, guess what? I found you another toad, and it is in the backyard in your bug catcher."
JJ ran to the back door, quickly opened the door, and ran outside to see the toad.

JJ exclaimed, "This is the best and biggest toad ever! I am going to call him Mr. Toad!" JJ was so excited that he immediately found a big bin to create the biggest and best aquarium for him.

JJ and his brother and sisters played with the toad all morning. They had a pool set up from the night before and placed him in it. Mr. Toad was swimming around, and everyone was laughing and enjoying Mr. Toad's every move.

As the day went on, JJ realized that maybe
Mr. Toad missed his family.
JJ asked his dad if he could bring him back to
the pond to find his family.
His dad looked down at him and said,
"Absolutely! Let's take him back now."
JJ and his dad walked down to
the pond together, and JJ placed Mr. Toad
onto a log on the edge of the pond and said,
"Thanks for playing with me, Mr. Toad. I
hope you find your friends and family."

You never know who will come into your life and make a difference. For JJ, Mr. Toad made a positive impact- one that he will never forget. Be a TOAD for someone today!

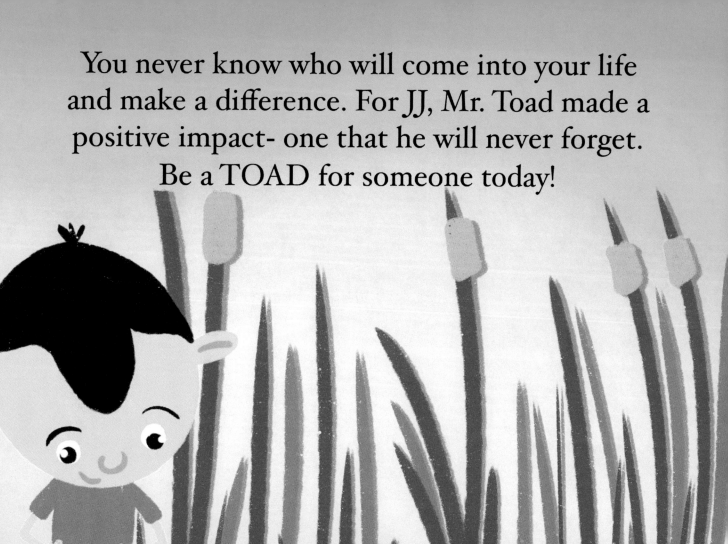

The end.

ABOUT THE AUTHOR

Joe Sweeney is a devoted husband, loving father, and accomplished educator with a passion for shaping young minds. Joe has dedicated nearly two decades of his professional life to the field of education. He spent almost a decade as a high school teacher, football coach, and dean of students; five years as an assistant principal; and is currently serving as a middle school principal. Joe firmly believes that education extends beyond textbooks and aims to create an inclusive and stimulating learning environment that empowers students to reach their full potential. He is currently pursuing his doctorate in educational leadership at the University of St. Francis in Joliet, Illinois.

Joe finds his greatest joy as a husband and father. He is married to his loving and supportive wife, Melissa, and together they have been blessed with four children: JJ, Mackenzie, Mia, and Ryan. Joe's experiences as a parent have deepened his understanding of the importance of a well-rounded education and its impact on shaping young lives.

As an educator and principal, he is driven by a genuine desire to make a positive difference in the lives of those he serves, inspiring students to embrace knowledge, grow personally, and live the mission of being a T.O.A.D.

FIND OUT MORE ABOUT AUTHOR JOE SWEENEY AND HOW TO BE A TOAD HERE!

Made in the USA
Monee, IL
14 August 2023

41009709R00024